FOX ON THE JOB

by James Marshall

DIAL BOOKS FOR YOUNG READERS · NEW YORK

Dial easy-to-read

For Clark Henley

Published by
Dial Books for Young Readers
A Division of Penguin Books USA Inc.
375 Hudson Street
New York, New York 10014

The Dial Easy-to-Read logo is a registered trademark of
Dial Books for Young Readers,
a Division of Penguin Books, USA Inc., ® TM 1,162,718.

Library of Congress Cataloging in Publication Data
Marshall, James, 1942- Fox on the job.
Summary: Fox tries to earn the money for a new
bicycle in several different jobs.
[1. Foxes–Fiction. 2. Humorous stories.] I. Title.
PZ7.M35672Fr 1988 [E] 87-15589
ISBN 0-8037-0350-3
ISBN 0-8037-0351-1 (lib. bdg.)

COBE
3 5 7 9 10 8 6 4

The art for each picture consists of an ink, pencil,
and watercolor painting, which is scanner-separated
and reproduced in full color.

Reading Level 2.0

Fox liked to show off
for the girls.

"Oh, my!" said the girls.

One day Fox showed off just

a little too much.

"Look out!" cried the girls.

"Look out!"

Fox was saved,

but his bike

was a wreck.

"That's all right,"

he told the girls.

"I'll just ask my mother

for a new one."

"Now, see here, Fox," said Mom.

"I'm not made of money.

You will just have to get a job

if you want a new bike."

"A job!" said Fox.

"There must be some other way."

And he went to his little sister.

"Louise, dear," said Fox.

But Louise would not help.

"I'll scream!" she said.

"I won't forget this,"
said Fox.

"Who needs a bike anyway?" said Fox.

Just then Carmen rode by.

"Tra-la!" sang Carmen.

"That does it!" said Fox.

And he went to look for a job.

NEW SHOES

Downtown Fox saw a sign

in a window.

HELP WANTED! NOW!

"I'm in luck," said Fox.

He went inside.

"Help is here!" he said.

"Not so fast," said the owner.

"Can you sell shoes?"

"Of course, I can," said Fox.

"Are you honest?" said the owner.

"Oh, yes!" said Fox.

"Well," said the owner.

"Let's give it a try.

You can start right away."

And he went to eat his lunch.

Fox kept himself busy.

"What an easy job," he said.

"Excuse me," said a lady.

"Can you help me?"

"That's what I'm here for,"
said Fox.
"I need some shoes,"
said the lady.
"Some pretty little pink ones."
Fox looked at the lady's feet.

16

"You can't mean it," he said.

"We may not *have* shoes that big.

Those are the biggest feet!"

"Well, I *never*!" cried the lady.

"What seems to be the trouble?"

said the owner.

"He said I have big feet!"

cried the lady.

"There, there," said the owner.

"Your feet are tiny."

And he turned to Fox.

"This is not the job for you."

"Well, I *never*!" said Fox.

THE
HAUNTED
HOUSE

Fox walked by

the amusement park.

"Too bad I don't have money

for a few rides," he said.

"I heard that," said Mr. Jones,

who ran the park.

"Perhaps you would like a job?"

"You don't mean it!"

said Fox.

Mr. Jones put Fox to work

at the Haunted House.

"What's inside?" said Fox.

"Oh, it's very scary,"

said Mr. Jones.

Fox's first customers were Carmen
and her little brother Clark.

"A ticket for the kid," said Carmen.

"Aren't you going in?" asked Fox.

"It's not scary enough," said Carmen.

Fox and Carmen waited and waited.

"What's taking that kid so long?"
said Fox.

"Maybe he got lost," said Carmen.

"Why don't you go inside
and look for him?"

"I beg your pardon?" said Fox.

"You aren't scared, are you?"

said Carmen.

"Me, scared?" said Fox.

And he went into the Haunted House.

Inside it was really something.

"Welcome to the Haunted House!"
cried a skeleton.

"I'm coming to get you!"
cried a ghost.

"Boo!" cried a vampire.

Poor Fox was as white as a sheet.

"Hi, Fox!" said Clark.

"I'll show you how to get out."

"For shame!" said Fox to Mr. Jones.
"That's no place for little kids!
I quit!"

"Oh, pooh," said Mr. Jones.
"They love it!"

PIZZA
TIME

Fox saw his friend Dexter

coming out of the pizza parlor.

"You can't fire *me*," said Dexter.

"I quit!"

"Fine," said the boss.

"Maybe my next delivery boy

won't eat up all the pizza!"

Dexter left in a huff.

And Fox stepped inside

the pizza parlor.

"Do you have a job for me?" asked Fox.

"Do you like pizza?" said the boss.

"I prefer hot dogs," said Fox.

"Excellent," said the boss.

"Are you fast on your feet?"

"Like the wind," said Fox.

"Excellent," said the boss.

"Take this pizza over to Mrs. O'Hara.
She has been waiting a long time."

Fox was out the door in a flash.

On Homer's Hill

Fox picked up speed.

"I'm the fastest fox in town,"

he said.

At that moment

Louise came around the corner.

She was taking her pet mice

to the vet for their shots.

It was quite a crash!

Fox, Louise, and everything else

went flying.

They saw stars.

"Now you've done it!" said Fox.

"You've made me late.

I'll really have to step on it!"

And he hurried away.

Louise went to the vet's.

Doctor Jane opened the box.

"Where are your pet mice?" she said.

"This looks like a pizza."

"Uh-oh," said Louise.

Fox knocked on Mrs. O'Hara's door.

"It's about time," said Mrs. O'Hara.

"I'm having a party.

And we're just dying for pizza."

"It will be worth the wait," said Fox.

"Pizza time!"

said Mrs. O'Hara to her friends.

She opened the box.

Back at the pizza parlor

the boss was hopping mad.

"Mrs. O'Hara just called," he said.

"And you are fired!"

"Didn't she like the pizza?" said Fox.

A
BRIGHT
IDEA

"This just isn't my day," said Fox.
"But I'm not giving up.
I'll think of something."

Just then he came to a furniture store.
And suddenly he had a bright idea.

"Business is bad, Fox,"
said the owner of the store.
"I can't give you a job."

"Maybe you can," said Fox.
And he told the owner his bright idea.

Later that day Carmen and Dexter
were out for a stroll.

"Look at that," said Dexter.

A large crowd was standing
in front of the furniture store.

"I can't see," said Carmen.

"Lift me up."

Dexter lifted Carmen above the crowd.

"What is going on?" said Dexter.

"It's Fox!" shouted Carmen.

"What a great bed!" said someone.

"I want one!" said someone else.

"What a great idea!" said the boss.

But Fox was already sound asleep—

and dreaming of his new bike.